Witch, Goblin, and Ghost
in the
Haunted Woods

Witch, Goblin, and Ghost

in the Haunted Woods

Five I AM READING *Stories*

by Sue Alexander
pictures by Jeanette Winter

Pantheon Books

For two very special people:
Lin Oliver and Steve Mooser

Library of Congress Cataloging in Publication Data
Alexander, Sue, 1933-
Witch, Goblin, and Ghost in the haunted woods.
(*An* I AM READING *Book*)
SUMMARY: Goblin, Ghost, and Witch look for buried treasure,
go swimming, play a game, hear a story,
and get lost in a snowstorm.
[1. Witches—Fiction. 2. Ghost stories]
I. Winter. Jeanette. II. Title.
PZ7.A3784Wg [E] 80-20863
ISBN 0-394-84443-2   ISBN 0-394-94443-7 (lib. bdg.)

THE STORIES

GOBLIN'S TREASURE

It was spring.

Goblin was cleaning his cave.

He found a book

he thought he'd lost.

He found a seashell

that Ghost had given him.

He found the two missing pieces

of his jigsaw puzzle.

And at the bottom of his closet

he found a map.

Goblin sneezed.

"This map must be very old,"

he said. "It's very dusty."

And he sneezed again.

Goblin looked at the map.

The Haunted Woods were on it.

The hills around his cave were on it.

The road past his cave was on it.

His cave was on the map, too.

And right in front of the cave

there was a big X.

"Oh!" Goblin said.

"X always marks the spot

where *treasure* is buried.

This must be a treasure map!"

Goblin got his shovel

and hurried outside.

He looked at the map.

Then he took three big steps.

"This looks like the right spot,"

Goblin said.

And he began to dig.

He dug and he dug and he dug.

But he didn't find any treasure.

"Hmmm," Goblin said.

He looked at the map again.

"Maybe that wasn't the right spot
after all," he said.

He took two more big steps
and began to dig.

He dug and dug and dug.

But he still didn't find
any treasure.
"This must not be
the right spot either!"
Goblin said.
So he took one more big step
and began to dig there.
He dug and dug and dug.
And this time
his shovel hit something!
"I've found it!" Goblin shouted.
"I've found the buried treasure!"

And he dug it up.

But it wasn't a treasure at all.

It was a big rock.

"Oh, no!" Goblin said.

He looked at the holes he had dug.

"Hmmm," he said.

"Maybe I'm not digging deep enough.

Maybe the treasure is buried

very, very deep."

Goblin began to dig again.

He dug deeper and deeper
and deeper.
But he still didn't find
any treasure.
"Digging for treasure
is very hard work!"
Goblin said.
And he sat down to rest.
Goblin looked
at all the holes he had dug.
He looked at the map again.

"I must still be digging
in the wrong spot," he said.
And he sighed.
Just then Witch and Ghost
came up the road.
"My goodness, Goblin!" Witch said.
"What are you doing?"
"I'm digging for treasure," Goblin said.
"Treasure?" said Ghost.
"Yes," Goblin said.
"A treasure was buried in my yard
a long time ago."

"How do you know, Goblin?" asked Witch.

"I found an old treasure map,"
Goblin said.
And he showed the map
to Witch and Ghost.

Then he began to dig again.

"Are you sure

this is a treasure map?" asked Ghost.

"It must be," Goblin said.

"It has an X on it.

And X always marks the spot
where treasure is buried."
"Well, it wasn't a treasure map
when I drew it," said Witch.
Goblin stopped digging.
"*You* drew this map, Witch?" he said.
"Yes," said Witch. "I did.
And this X marks the spot
where you were going
to plant a garden. You forgot."
Goblin turned
an embarrassed shade of pink.

Ghost looked at all the holes

that Goblin had dug.

"It may not have been

a treasure map," said Ghost.

"But it *can* be one."

"What do you mean?" Goblin asked.

"You could plant

a very big garden now," Ghost said.

"Yes," said Witch.

"And then you would have

a *real* treasure."

Goblin looked at his yard.

"That's true," he said.

"I could plant

lots of flowers and vegetables now!"

And that's just what he did.

THE LAKE

One hot summer day

Witch, Goblin, and Ghost

were trying to keep cool.

"I have an idea," said Ghost.

"Let's go down to the lake.

It's much cooler there."

"That's a good idea, Ghost,"

Witch said.

Goblin thought so too.

They packed a lunch.
Ghost took his fishing pole.

Witch took her sketch pad.

Goblin took the book
he was reading.

And off they went.
"Ah! This is much better!" said Ghost
when they got to the lake.
"Feel that cool breeze!"
"It does feel good," Goblin said.

"Look!" said Witch.

"There are ducks swimming in the lake!"

"I'm going swimming too!" Ghost said.

"Me too!" said Witch.

And they ran into the water.

"Come on, Goblin!" Ghost called.

Goblin looked at the lake.

It looked deep.

Goblin thought for a minute.

Then he said, "I don't want
to go swimming right now.

I'm at a very interesting place
in my book.
I want to read for a while."
"Then come and swim
when you're finished reading,"
Witch said.
Goblin watched Witch and Ghost.
Ghost was swimming on his side.
Witch was floating on her back.
They looked like they were having
a very good time.

Goblin sighed.

After a while Witch and Ghost

came out of the water.

"Come on in, Goblin," said Ghost.

"The water feels good."

Goblin looked at the lake again.

It looked deep.

It looked too deep to stand in.

"I don't want to go swimming

right now," Goblin said.

"It's time for lunch. Let's eat."

Ghost frowned.

"I'd rather swim," he said.

"It *is* almost lunchtime," said Witch.

"Oh, all right," said Ghost.

Goblin opened the lunch basket.

And they ate.

When they were finished Ghost said,

"Let's go swimming!"

"We can't, Ghost," Goblin said.

"We have to wait for a while."

"That's true," Witch said.

"It isn't safe to go swimming
right after you eat."

Ghost sighed.

"You're right, Witch," he said.

"We will have to wait."

"I think I'll draw for a while,"
Witch said.

"I'll see if I can draw the ducks
swimming in the lake."

And she picked up her sketch pad.

Ghost picked up his fishing pole.

"I'll see if I can catch some fish,"
he said.

And he went down to
the grassy edge of the lake.

Witch drew.

Ghost fished.

And Goblin read.

After a long while Ghost said,

"It must be all right

to go swimming *now*."

"Yes," said Witch. "I think it is."

"Good," said Ghost. "Let's go!"

Ghost and Witch ran into the water.

"Come on, Goblin!" Ghost called.

21

Goblin looked at the lake.

It looked very, very deep.

"I–I can't, Ghost!" he called back.

"My toe hurts."

Ghost and Witch came out of the water.

They looked at Goblin's toe.

"I don't see anything wrong

with your toe, Goblin," Witch said.

"Neither do I," said Ghost.

"Well, it hurts," Goblin said.

"I think I'd better not go swimming.

Maybe my toe will be better

next summer."

Witch and Ghost didn't say anything.

They just looked at Goblin.

Then Ghost said,

"I think I'll tell a story."

"Oh, good!" Goblin said.

"Once there was a goblin," said Ghost,

"who wouldn't swim in the lake.

First he said he wanted to read.

Then he said he was hungry.

And then he said his toe hurt.

Now this goblin had two good friends.

They had a feeling

that the goblin was afraid of the water

because he didn't know how to swim.

So they decided to teach him.

The end."

Goblin turned a blushing shade of rose.

"I like that story, Ghost," he said.

"Then let's go in the water,"
Ghost said.

Goblin looked at the lake.

Then he looked at Witch and Ghost.

"All right," he said.

And they all went
down to the lake together.

Witch and Ghost showed Goblin

how to blow bubbles in the water.

They showed him

how to float on his back.

And then they showed him

how to swim on his side.

Goblin had a very good time.

"You know what, Witch?" he said.

"You know what, Ghost?

The water is deep

but swimming is fun!"

And Witch and Ghost agreed.

THE GAME

Witch and Goblin were sitting
on Witch's porch.
"Witch," Goblin said,
"let's play hide-and-seek
in the meadow."
"That sounds like a good thing to do,"
Witch said.
So off they went to the meadow.

"You close your eyes, Goblin,"
Witch said, "and I'll hide."
"All right," Goblin said.
Goblin closed his eyes.
He began to count, "One, two, three . . ."
Witch hid.
Goblin counted up to ten.
Then he opened his eyes.
"Here I come, Witch!" he called.
"Ready or not!"
Goblin went to look for Witch.

He looked behind a big tree.

Witch wasn't there.

He looked behind a pile of rocks.

Witch wasn't there.

He looked in the patch of sunflowers.

And there she was!

"I found you, Witch!" Goblin yelled.

And he laughed.

"Now it's my turn to hide,"

Goblin said.

"You close *your* eyes, Witch."

Witch closed her eyes.

She began to count, "One, two, three . . ."

Goblin looked for a place to hide.

He went by the big tree.

He went past the pile of rocks.

He went through the sunflower patch.

Then he saw a hollow log.

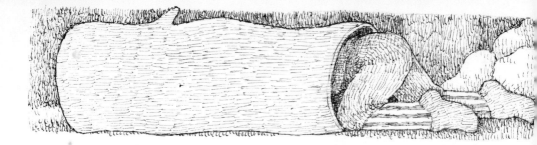

"That looks like

a good place to hide," Goblin said.

And he crawled inside the log.

Goblin heard Witch count up to ten.

Then he heard Witch say,

"Here I come, Goblin! Ready or not!"

Goblin laughed.

"Witch will look behind the big tree,"

he said. "But she won't find me!"

He peeked out of the log.

He saw the big tree.

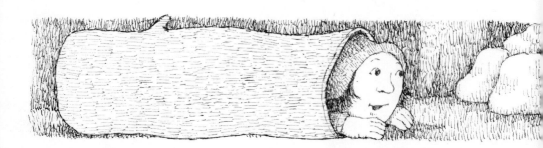

But he didn't see Witch.

"Witch must be looking

behind the big rocks," Goblin said.

"But she won't find me there!"

Goblin peeked out of the log again.

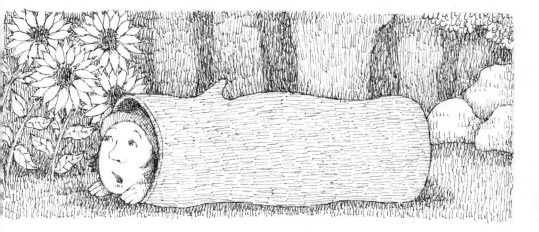

He saw the pile of rocks.

He saw the sunflower patch.

But he didn't see Witch.

"Hmmm," Goblin said,

"I wonder where she went

to look for me!"

He lay down inside the log.

"Maybe Witch went far away

to look for me," Goblin thought.

"Maybe it will take a while

for her to find me."

Goblin waited.

He heard a bird singing.

He heard some crickets.

But he didn't hear Witch.

"Witch is taking a *very* long time

to find me!" Goblin thought.

He rolled over inside the log.

He heard the breeze

rustle the meadow grass.

He heard some bees going by.

But he didn't hear Witch.

"Maybe Witch isn't going to come!"

he thought.

"Maybe she will *never* find me!"

And he began to cry.

Just then Goblin heard footsteps.

He felt the log go *bump!*

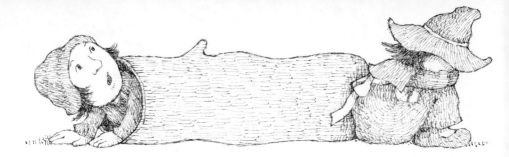

Then he heard Witch say, "Oh dear,

I can't find Goblin anywhere!

He wasn't behind the big tree.

He wasn't behind the rocks.

And he wasn't in the sunflower patch.

I don't know where he can be!"

And she sniffled.

Goblin wiped his eyes.

He poked his head out of the log.

"Here I am, Witch!" he said.

Witch jumped up.

"Oh, Goblin!

I'm so glad to see you!" she said.

"I was afraid I would never find you!"

Goblin came out of the log.

"I was afraid of that, too, Witch,"

he said.

And he thought for a minute.

Then he said, "You know what, Witch?

We *both* won this game.

We found each other!"

"So we did, Goblin," Witch said.

"So we did."

GHOST'S STORY

One autumn evening
Ghost and Goblin
were in Ghost's tree.
"Ghost," Goblin said,
"how about telling a story?"
"All right," said Ghost.
"What kind of a story
would you like to hear?"
Goblin looked outside.

The wind was rustling

through the trees.

The moving branches were making

spidery shadows on the ground.

And the moon had an orange glow.

"It's the right kind of night

for a scary story," Goblin said.

Ghost looked outside.

"Hmmm. So it is," he said.

And he thought for a moment.

Goblin curled up in the chair.

"Once upon a time," Ghost said,

"a goblin went for a walk.

And a monster caught him.

The monster took the goblin

to the monster palace

at the top of the mountain.

"I'm going to eat you!"

roared the monster.

"Wouldn't you like

a nice roasted turkey instead?"

asked the goblin.

"That sounds good," said the monster.

"Cook it for me!"

So the goblin roasted a big turkey.

He made mashed potatoes.

And he made a big chocolate cake.

The monster ate it all up.

And as he ate, he got bigger.

"I'm still hungry!"

roared the monster.

"Now I'll eat YOU!"

"Wouldn't you like

some nice baked ham instead?"

asked the goblin.

"That sounds good," said the monster.

"Cook it for me!"

So the goblin baked two big hams,

five big yams,

and two lemon pies.

"That's more like it!"

roared the monster.

And he ate everything all up.

And as he ate,

he got bigger and bigger.

"I'm still hungry!"

roared the monster.

"Now I'm going to eat you!"

"Wouldn't you like

some nice roast beef instead?"

asked the goblin.

"That *does* sound good,"

said the monster.

"Cook it for me!"

So the goblin roasted

seven roast beefs,

twenty ears of corn,

and made five cherry pies.

"Ahhhhh!" sighed the monster.

And he ate everything all up.

And as he ate, he got bigger
and bigger and bigger.

He got bigger than the chair.

He got bigger than the table.

He got bigger than anything
the goblin had ever seen.

"I think I'd better go now,"
said the goblin.
"No you don't!" roared the monster.
"I'm STILL going to eat you!"
And he ran after the goblin.
But he was too big
to get through the door.
"I'm stuck!" roared the monster.
"Good!" shouted the goblin.
And the goblin ran
out of the monster palace,
down the mountain
and far, far away.
And for all we know,
the monster is still stuck in the door.
The end."

Goblin shivered.

"That *was* a scary story," he said.

"But you know what, Ghost?

It was a *hungry* story too."

"Hmmm," said Ghost.

"You're right, Goblin."

So Ghost and Goblin each ate

two apples,

three pieces of fudge

and drank four glasses of lemonade.

THE SNOWSTORM

Goblin looked outside.

All the hills had snow caps.

There were icicles on the trees.

And snowflakes were swirling

through the air.

"Hmmm," said Goblin.

"It's snowing *very* hard.

I think I'll stay inside."

He got his big warm quilt.

He took a pile of books

from his bookcase.

And he curled up in his chair to read.

Goblin read for a very long time.

Then he began to yawn.

"Maybe I should rest for a minute,"

he said.

Goblin closed his eyes.

And he fell fast asleep.

While he was asleep he had a dream.

He dreamed that he was in

the Haunted Woods.

The snow was swirling all around him.

He could not see the trees.

He could not see the bushes.

He could not see the path.

And he could not find his way home.

"I'm lost!" Goblin cried.

Just then Ghost came

into Goblin's dream.

"Don't worry, Goblin," said Ghost.

"Follow me and I will lead you home."

Ghost started off.

Goblin followed him.

Snow swirled all around them.

"Ghost, don't go so fast!"

Goblin called.

"I cannot see to follow you!"

But Ghost didn't answer.

The snow swirled harder.

And Ghost disappeared.

"Oh no!" Goblin cried.

"Ghost is gone! I'm still lost!"

Goblin tried to see

through the swirling snow.

"Maybe the path is *this* way," he said.

And he started off.

Snow swirled all around him.

Goblin could not see

where he was going.

He could not see where he had been.

He could not see up.

He could not see down.

SMMUSSH! PLOP!

Goblin tumbled into a snowdrift!

"Oh no!" he cried.

"Now I'll never get home!"

Just then Witch came

into Goblin's dream.

"Don't worry, Goblin," Witch said.

"Climb on my broomstick.

I will take you home."

Goblin climbed on Witch's broomstick.

Witch made the broomstick
go high into the sky.
Snow swirled all around them.
"Witch, don't fly so high!"
Goblin called.
"I will fall off!"
But Witch didn't answer.
The broomstick went higher
and higher
and higher.
And Goblin fell off.
He fell down—
and down—
and down.
And he landed with a THUMP!
"Oh no!" Goblin cried.

Just then someone called his name.

Goblin opened his eyes

and looked around.

He was not in the Haunted Woods.

He was not in a swirling snowstorm.

And he was not lost.

He was in his cave.

He had only fallen out of his chair.

And Witch was calling his name.

"Goblin!" Witch called again.

"Are you there?"

Goblin rubbed his eyes.

Then he got up and let Witch in.

Ghost was with her.

"Oh Witch! Oh Ghost!

I'm so glad to see you!" Goblin said.

And he shivered.

"What's the matter, Goblin?"

asked Witch.

"I fell asleep

and had a terrible dream,"

Goblin said.

"I dreamed I was lost

in a swirling snowstorm.

I dreamed that

you were going to lead me home, Ghost.

But you disappeared instead.

Then I dreamed

you were going to take me home

on your broomstick, Witch.

But you flew too high and I fell off.

And I was *still* lost!"

"That *was* a terrible dream, Goblin,"

Ghost said.

"But if you were lost in a snowstorm,

I would not disappear."

"And I would not let you

fall off my broomstick," Witch said.

"And we would not let you stay lost,"
said Ghost.

"No," said Witch. "We wouldn't."

Goblin turned a glad shade of pink.

Then he looked outside.

"Witch! Ghost!" he said. "Look!

It has stopped snowing.

We can go out and play!"

And that's what they did.

SUE ALEXANDER is the author of ten highly praised books for children, including *Witch, Goblin, and Sometimes Ghost; More Witch, Goblin, and Ghost Stories*; and *Seymour, the Prince (Pantheon* I AM READING *Books)*. She is on the board of directors of the Society of Children's Book Writers and was given the 1980 Dorothy C. McKenzie Award by the Southern California Council on Literature for Children. She has three grown children and lives with her husband in Canoga Park, California.

JEANETTE WINTER's first picture book, *The Christmas Visitors*, was published by Pantheon in 1968. It was an AIGA Children's Book of the Year and features the same delicate impishness and droll humor that have endeared Witch, Goblin, and Ghost to children everywhere. She is also the illustrator of *Harry (the Monster)* by Ann Cameron. She lives with her husband and their two sons in Dallas, Texas.